Lickin' Larry and the Search For Peanut Butter & Rock Ice Cream

By

Bernard Aleman

For My Aubree.

The story you are about to read
Is unlike any other book,

For the pages within
Hold no pictures
Upon which you can look,

The words will paint them
In your head and in your heart,
So on blank pages within
You may create your own art!

There shall be no right
And there shall be no wrong,
Because the pictures in you
Shall write their own song,

This tale will become solely yours
In that very special way,
And this will remain true
Day after day after day,

To you I now give a story
Of kindness, adventure, kinship, & care
Penned in sincerest love,
That you may share,

Give its grace freely
To all whom you do and don't know,
For that is what the spirit
Of Lickin' Larry most absolutely glows!

Chapter 1: The Little Lizard

Lickin' Larry was a little mountain lizard and a quite handsome one at that. His skin was green as emeralds and his eyes were as brown as cinnamon sticks. But nothing was as beautiful as his generous heart. He lived in a wonderful little mountain cabin near a wonderful little village called Tiny Town.

Lickin' Larry never had anything bad to say about anyone. He always did his best to recognize the good in others and always shared whatever he had with whoever needed it. He was an all-around good, lizard fellow and that is why he had many, many friends who enjoyed his company.

His most favorite thing in the world was sharing his most favorite dessert in the world with those whose company he enjoyed the most; and they were any one of his many friends.

What was his most favorite dessert in the world you ask? Well, it was Peanut Butter & Rock ice cream of course! Lickin' Larry just loved the smooth creamy taste of the extra peanut buttery, peanut butter and the super crunchety-crunch of the itty, bitty rock candies mixed inside.

They were every color of the rainbow and sparkled like little diamonds stuck in ice cream when the sunlight hit them; every day he worked hard so that he could reward himself with a scoop or two of this most special of treats.

One particular sunny Sunday, Lickin' Larry was out in his garden working quite hard planting yummy fruit and vegetable seeds. It was a well-known fact that he was an excellent gardener. You could say he had a very good green thumb.

I know what you are thinking. "*But he already has green thumbs...he's a green lizard!"* What I mean is that he had a special talent for gardening. Anything he planted grew and grew and grew. His favorites were giant tomatoes, potatoes, carrots, honeydew melons and big, fat, giant strawberries.

Every year at harvest time, Lickin' Larry always shared his bounty with his friends. They would help him gather his gigantic fruits and vegetables and he would prepare a grand feast for them all. This great, big food celebration came to be known as Lickin' Larry's Large La-La-La and every year everybody in Tiny Town always looked forward to it.

Anyhow, that's what Lickin' Larry was doing that Sunday, getting ready for the Large La-La-La and it had been very difficult work indeed. He had been planting seeds since early that morning and now at noon he was finally done. "I think I deserve three scoops today!" he said as he skipped out of the garden and into the cozy, little kitchen of his wonderful, mountain cabin. With a smile so wide all of his pearly white teeth showed he grabbed hold of the refrigerator door, swung it open and snatched the container of Peanut Butter & Rock ice cream. His little lizard fingers worked fast to free his most favorite dessert in the world from its ice cream prison.

But when Lickin' Larry opened it he was saddened to find that the container was empty.

"Oh, me! Oh, my! I must have eaten the last of it yesterday when Johnny Jump-up stopped by." And just like that Lickin' Larry's little lizard mind wandered into his memories of the day before.

Chapter 2: Johnny Jump-Up

It had been a very beautiful day yesterday. The sun smiled sweet sunshine all over the valley and puffy, white clouds swam across the sky making funny shapes as they traveled by. Lickin' Larry was just enjoying the Saturday. He sat on his rickety old rocking chair with his little lizard feet propped up on the porch railing and chewed away at a crispy, green apple.

Crunch, munch, munch...crunch, munch, munch...crunch, munch, munch went the sound of the crispy green apple as it disappeared into his hungry, green belly. Mmmmmmmmmm...

went the sound escaping his mouth as he tasted the yummy piece of fruit. "Life is good," he thought to himself.

After he was done devouring the delicious dessert his eyes began to grow heavy with sleep. "Time for a nap," he said in his head. Like a lion roaring in the jungle he bellowed an enormous yawn, stretched like he had never stretched before and got comfortable in his rickety, old rocking chair. As his little lizard self was drifting off into the land of dazzling dreams he heard a very loud shout.

"Yeeehaaaaw!! I did it!!" The voice echoed up the trail like a booming bomb and exploded straight into his ears. "What the...? Who...? Where in the..." Lickin' Larry snorted as he was startled out of his very short nap.

He sat up in a flash and feverishly looked around this way and that trying to find where the mysterious voice had come from. Up, down, and all around his eyes went until finally he saw something coming towards his little, log cabin.

As the something got closer and closer Lickin' Larry's little lizard eyes got wider and wider. Very soon he knew exactly what that something was, "Why it's my very good grasshopper- friend

Johnny Jump-Up!"

Johnny was pop, pop, popping along in this direction and that like superheated popcorn-kernel-missiles rocketing towards the sky. He was whooping and hollering, "I did it! I did it! Yippeee! I did it!" Lickin' Larry noticed his grasshopper friend's obvious elation and asked, "Wow, what's up Johnny?!"

Johnny came to a dead stop right at Lickin' Larry's doorstep, took a moment to catch his breath and said, "Larry, Larry, I did it! I just found out that I passed my last exam at Tiny Town University which means I have earned my teaching certificate and that means I am going to get to be a teacher!!"

"Congratulations, Johnny! I knew you could do it! All your hard work has paid off again!" Lickin' Larry said to his grasshopper-friend.

He knew that Johnny's dream had always been to become an educator ever since their third grade teacher had gone out of her way to help his friend.

Her name was Ms. Lady Bugg and she was the kind of teacher that we should all be lucky enough to have. Ms. Lady Bugg truly cared for all of her students.

As a little grasshopper Johnny had

had a difficult time in school, but it was not because he had been a poor student and did not pay attention. There was something else going on.

It was Ms. Lady Bugg who had first noticed something was different about Johnny. She did not believe that he was just not a good student and so she began to spend extra time with him every day after school.

She tested Johnny's abilities until she discovered what his problem was. It turned out that Johnny's mind worked slightly different than most others'. His brain could learn just as much as any other brain, but it just had to learn it in a slightly different way.

Ms. Lady Bugg helped and helped Johnny to learn how to retrain his brain and very soon his mind became like a great, big sponge of intelligence absorbing every bit of knowledge he could.

With his newfound confidence and with Ms. Lady Bugg constantly encouraging him it was not long before Johnny went from being a poor student to being the best student in the whole school.

"I am so very proud of you, Johnny. You never gave up even when that is what you said you really wanted to do.

You worked and you worked to achieve your goals and that is the best chance you can give yourself. Students like you are the reason I will always be a teacher," Ms. Lady Bugg would say to her favorite grass-hopper student (he was her only one).

Johnny Jump-Up would respond in kind, "And you are the reason I know what I want to do when I grow up. I will be a teacher so that I might be able to pass on to others all the kindness, patience, and compassion you have given me. Thank you, Ms. Lady Bugg for everything you have done for me and thank you for always believing in me."

As Lickin' Larry finished remembering Johnny's visit yesterday he was happy for his friend all over again. He felt selfish for having been upset by the fact that he was out of Peanut Butter & Rock ice cream.

"How silly of me..." he said to himself, "Johnny's going to get to make his dream come true and I'm worried about ice cream. There's absolutely no need for me to be sad at all. I had the privilege of sharing in his happiness yesterday and that is what matters. And even though I am still really wanting some super-crunchety, extra peanut-buttery, Peanut Butter & Rock ice cream I am not going to be upset that I do not have any because I can just go to the store and get more."

With a smile as bright as sunshine stretching across his little lizard face he grabbed his floppy gardening hat and trusty walking stick and set off over the river and through the woods; to Tiny Town he went because that is where more Peanut Butter & Rock ice cream was waiting.

Chapter 3: Tiny Town

It did not take him long to get there. The dirt street was soft on his little lizard feet. It was like he was walking on a not-too-bouncy balloon and Tiny Town was abuzz with the hustle and bustle of the many, many town's folk who were there doing everything.

At Catie Caterpillar's Clothes Shoppe they were trying on fancy new duds. Through the windows of the Bank of Tiny Town he could see folks doing bank stuff. Inside Billie Butterfly's Beauty Salon ladies were getting their antennas done.

On and on Lickin' Larry strolled down Main Street delighting in the very beautiful sights and sounds that made up Tiny Town. "I just love the way everyone here is so respectful and polite to one another. I am glad to be part of such a wonderful community," he thought to himself.

And just as he finished thinking this a pleasant surprise grabbed his attention, "So nice to see you Lickin' Larry! How are you?" said Mrs. Mary Mouse. She was sitting on the outside patio of Antonio Ant's Tea Time Restaurant.

Remembering his manners Lickin'

Larry replied, "I am fine today. Thank you for asking, Mrs. Mouse. And how are you?"

Mrs. Mary Mouse who was always in the mood for a good visit said, "Today is beautiful and I feel beautiful, inside and out. Will you please join me for some tea and cookies?"

Lickin' Larry being the good lizard fellow that he always was answered, "Any other day I would very much like to join you, but you see, today I've finally finished planting my seeds for this year's Large La-La-La and I'm on my way to Sammy Spider's Store to buy Peanut Butter & Rock ice cream to celebrate the occasion."

Mrs. Mary Mouse suddenly remembered just how much Peanut Butter & Rock ice cream meant to Lickin' Larry and said, "Why that's glorious news! You should be very proud of yourself! I shall talk to you another time then. Have a nice day."

"Mrs. Mouse..." said Lickin' Larry, "You are a gem of a soul indeed. Thank you for understanding. I shall see you again very soon. Bye." And off he strolled towards the opposite end of Tiny Town because that is exactly where Sammy Spider's Store was.

With each little lizard step he knew

he was getting closer to his most favorite dessert in the world. "It won't be long now! I can already taste that extra peanut-buttery, peanut butter and hear that super-crunchety-crunch crunch of those rainbow-sweet, ice cream diamonds!" Lickin' Larry rejoiced.

His leisurely walk quickly turned into a brisk run. Slappity, slap, slap... slappity, slap, slap went the beat of his fast little lizard feet hitting the soft-packed soil of Main Street as he hurried to buy his favorite treat.

He was soon at the front door of Sammy Spider's Store. He took a moment to catch his breath and then gently pushed open the creaky, wooden screen door. The bell hanging from above sang a small song and announced his arrival.

"Well, if it isn't my good friend, Lickin' Larry! How have you been? I haven't seen you in some time!" said Sammy Spider as he sat behind the counter reading a book. It was called <u>A Buck and a Quarter a Cow: The Story of Little Carlo Bolo</u>.

"I have been very good Sammy. And how are you? Hey, have you been working out? You look good! You are a lot more muscly since the last time I was here and what is that book you are reading anyway?" replied Lickin' Larry.

Sammy Spider said, "Well I have been riding my bike to and from the store every day for about a month now. I don't know that it's making my muscles bigger, but getting more exercise sure has made me feel better. As for the book it's about a little human boy who always has strange and interesting things happening to him. It's very good. You should read it sometime. I'll let you have it when I am done with it."

"Thank you Sammy I would appreciate having it especially since you recommended it. My goodness...you are incredible!" Lickin' Larry told his spider-friend. "What do you mean?" inquired Sammy.

"Well, not only are you keeping your body healthy by exercising, but you are also keeping your mind strong by reading. That is what I mean. Keep up the good work!" Lickin' Larry encouraged his friend.

Sammy Spider replied, "I will and thank you for your supportive friendship" and he added, "So, what brings you into Tiny Town today?"

Lickin' Larry started by saying, "Well Sammy I just spent a good long morning working extra hard preparing for this year's Large La-La-La and you know me...afterwards I wanted to reward myself with some of my most favorite dessert in the world..."

"Peanut Butter & Rock ice cream?" interrupted Sammy Spider. "That is correct!" exclaimed Lickin' Larry and he continued, "anyway...I noticed I was out and that is why I am here."

"You have come to the right place my friend," said Sammy Spider. "I just got a new delivery this morning. Help yourself. You know where to look."

The excitement was too much for Lickin' Larry. His most favorite dessert in the world was now close at hand and he could not contain himself.

His tongue began to dance outside of his mouth. It swirled left and it swirled right. His little lizard legs twitched like he had ants in his pants and his little lizard hands and fingers twirled around each other like tiny, turbulent tornadoes.

Down the aisle he glided toward the back of the store until he stood before the mighty freezer on the floor. Sammy had nicknamed it Samson. Lickin' Larry lifted Samson's heavy steel door and was blasted with a rush of very, very cold air. It was so cold that he thought he might freeze to death.

Long, pointy icicles began to grow on his little lizard face and soon he had a shiny beard of ice. It was so cold he had to shut Samson's steel door. "Whoa! It's like the North Pole in there! I need some help," concluded Lickin' Larry.

He ran back to the front of the store where his spider-friend was still reading his book. Sammy looked up as he heard Lickin' Larry coming. "What happened to you?" he asked his little lizard-friend.

"That freezer is freezing!" exclaimed Lickin' Larry. Sammy Spider joked, "Yeah, I know. It's a freezer and that's what it does." The two friends laughed and then Lickin' Larry

asked, "Say Sammy do you have a winter coat and some mittens?"

"Why I sure do. Let me get them for you," said Sammy Spider. He reached under the counter and pulled out a big and fluffy yellow coat with a huge hood along with a pair of kittens. Lickin' Larry put on the fluffy yellow coat, but then paused when he saw the kittens. "I said mittens Sammy not kittens!" smiled Lickin' Larry.

"Oh! I was wondering how kittens were going to help you in the freezer. Let me just put them back. Here you go…one pair of red mittens. Is that all?"

finished Sammy Spider. "Yes, I think I

am good to go!" exclaimed Lickin' Larry.

Chapter 4: BRRRRRR!!!!

He looked like a yellow, marshmallow snowman with red puffy hands as he opened Samson's mighty steel door and was blasted by the cold, cold air once again. Into the freezer he climbed and vanished into the white, icy landscape. "Peanut Butter & Rock ice cream here I come!" he shouted to the world.

The winds howled like a family of wolves calling to a full moon. They swirled around him from all directions and jostled his little lizard body like a boxer pounding on a punching bag. It was tough going, but Lickin' Larry was determined to be tougher.

Mountains of ice cream buckets surrounded him and little by little he was able to read their flavors. There was Gumshoe Grape, Amazing Apple, Mysterious Mint, Blushing Banana, Tons O' Chunks Chocolate, Stupendous Strawberry, and Valiant Vanilla.

He searched and searched for his most favorite dessert in the world, but he could not find it. Up and over buckets he climbed. Into caverns of ice cream he crept. He tried and he tried yet still he could not find any Peanut Butter & Rock ice cream.

Lickin' Larry had soon explored every nook and cranny of the icy terrain. "There isn't any here," he concluded disappointingly. He made his way back to Samson's mighty steel door, climbed out of the freezer and headed back to the front of the store.

Sammy Spider lifted all eight of his eyes from his book and saw his little lizard-friend approaching.

"You're back! I was beginning to get worried. Did Samson give you a hard time? How many buckets of Peanut Butter & Rock ice cream shall I ring you up for?" he asked.

Lickin' Larry replied, "Zero. I could not find any. I looked everywhere, but there was nothing of my most favorite dessert." Sammy Spider looked bewildered. He scratched his head and said, "Why, that can't be right. There should be some in there. Let me check my inventory book."

He reached below him, fumbled around a bit, pulled out a dusty, old book and thumped it on the counter. He then reached into his pocket and took out his glasses. And yes they fit all eight of his eyes.

Sammy Spider began to flip the pages until he got to the one he was looking for. "Let me see...hmmmm....ok...ok...oh no!" he declared. Lickin' Larry curious as to what his spider-friend had found asked, "What is the matter?"

Sammy Spider answered, "I see what happened. I placed the new orders for all the ice cream flavors last week and was told that the Peanut Butter & Rock ice cream machine was broken. The ice cream man said that I wouldn't be able to order anymore until it was fixed."

"Well, when is that going to be?" inquired Lickin' Larry. "Not for another week," responded Sammy Spider. He added, "I'm sorry. I thought I had some left because Johnny Jump-Up was in here earlier and bought two buckets.

He must have gotten the last two."

Lickin' Larry surprised to hear that his grasshopper-friend had stopped by wondered, "Johnny was here? He bought the last two buckets of Peanut Butter & Rock ice cream? How long ago did he leave? Which way did he go?"

Sammy Spider noticed his little lizard-friend's obvious excitement and said, "He left about thirty minutes ago and he said he was going home." Lickin' Larry's little lizard eyes lit up like a pitch-black room full of fireflies and he shouted, "Thanks Sammy! You are a life saver!" He grabbed his floppy gardening hat and out of Sammy

Spider's Store he zoomed like a faster-than-anything racecar. He forgot his trusty walking stick.

His little lizard legs spun round and round like he had his very own set of wheels. His little lizard arms pumped feverishly back and forth like powerful pistons. He was a blur of green as he sped out of Tiny Town. Lickin' Larry was a little lizard on another mission and that was to find his good grasshopper-friend Johnny Jump-Up.

Chapter 5: Colors, Colors, Colors and a Bump in the Road

He soon reached Petunia Pass and was stunned by the beauty of the valley below. Everywhere he looked vibrant colors splashed across the land and throughout the heavens above.

The smiling, yellow sun hovered happily in the mostly baby-blue sky. Fat, cotton clouds drifted and twisted around and around like graceful ballerinas.

The green branches of the tall, tall pine trees and the brown blades of the long prairie grasses danced this way and that in the gentle breeze.

The purples, reds, oranges, and

whites of the wonderful wild flowers carpeted the valley floor. The entire valley looked as if an army of rainbows had fallen from the sky and had painted it with all the colors of the universe. "Wow, that is magical," Lickin' Larry whispered to himself.

Down and down Petunia Pass he continued. Bumblebees buzzed in and out of the many, many wild flowers and everywhere crickets chirped all around him. Way up high in the big, blue, sky birds soared and sang the songs of Mother Nature.

Step after little lizard step Lickin' Larry found himself becoming lost in the natural music of the earth. His eyes soaked in sensational sights, his ears corralled incredible sounds, and his nose smelled sweet scents. Like a sponge he soaked in all the beauty the world had to offer.

In fact he was doing such a good job of appreciating it all that he did not notice the very large object right smack in the middle of the path and bumped right into it. Umph! Went the sound escaping Lickin' Larry's little lungs.

"What in the wide world is this?" he pondered. The object was furry, brown, and... breathing. As he looked closely he was hit with the realization that he knew what, or more to the point who, the object was. "Why it is my good friend Kablewy Bear!" Lickin' Larry said to himself. "But what is he doing right here?" he wondered out loud.

His question was answered the moment he heard several loud snores coming from Kablewy Bear's super-duper snout. "Ohhhh, he is sleeping. Well, that is okay because I am in a hurry anyway," Lickin' Larry said and started to make his way quietly around his sleeping bear-friend.

Getting passed Kablewy Bear turned into an adventure itself. Lickin' Larry did his best to be as quiet as possible.

He did not want to wake his bear-friend because he looked so peaceful.

He tried crawling through the long prairie grasses, but became scared that he might not find Petunia Pass again.

He tried climbing to the top of the grass so he could swing from blade to blade to get passed his bear-friend that way, but that did not work either. He was too heavy and the grass just bent the further up he climbed; like a bat in a cave Lickin' Larry was left dangling upside down each time with nowhere to go, but headfirst into the dirt.

After that he was left with only one more choice. "I guess I will have to climb over him," he said in his head. And so began his journey up and over the furry mountain called Kablewy Bear.

Now...you might be thinking that Lickin' Larry probably had a difficult time climbing his bear-friend. The truth of the matter was that he really had no trouble at all. You see lizards are excellent climbers. Their little lizard hands and little lizard feet have little claws that make it quite easy to climb almost anything...even big, snoring, sleeping bears.

Slowly and surely Lickin' Larry made his way onto his bear-friend's thick, brown fur. Up and over Kablewy's hiney, then across his back he went. The snores coming from the bear's super-duper snout became louder and louder. They made Kablewy's body tremble like he was a living, breathing earthquake.

As he climbed over and down his bear-friend's shoulder Lickin' Larry allowed himself to be hopeful. "Almost done," he said to himself. He could see Petunia Path straight ahead, "Just a little more to go... Peanut Butter & Rock ice cream here I come again!" he delighted as he crossed in front of Kablewy Bear's nose. BIG MISTAKE!

The instant Lickin' Larry stepped in front of Kablewy Bear's super-duper snout he was sucked in by its powerful forces and then...SPLAT went the sound of his little lizard body hitting the bear's wet and slimy nostrils. Kablewy sprang into action because he could not breathe.

He jumped up like a mighty kangaroo and began swatting at the air as if an army of bees was launching a surprise attack. He kept his eyes closed for fear that they might sting his eyeballs. After a few seconds Kablewy Bear slowly opened his eyes and was shocked to see something stuck to end of his super-duper snout. Like a doctor gently plucking a splinter out your skin Kawblewy Bear reached for the it stuck to the end of his nose and slowly peeled it away.

It was dripping wet with big, bear-snot. He carefully wiped it clean with his humongous paw. Little by little the identity of the something was revealed. "Lickin' Larry? What's up buddy? How are ya? What are up to? Were you trying to pick my nose?" Kablewy Bear asked curiously.

Breathing very heavily Lickin' Larry responded, "Hhhhhh...hhhhh....hi, Kablewy. No, I was not trying to pick your nose. I was trying to get over you so that I continue my search." Kablewy then inquired, "What are you searching for?"

"I am on a quest to find my most favorite dessert in the world," said Lickin' Larry. "Why were you looking for it in my nose? I don't have any Peanut Butter & Rock ice cream in there," Kablewy answered.

"I was not looking for it in your nose, Kawblewy! Johnny Jump-Up has it and I am on my way to his house to ask if he will share some with me," Lickin' Larry said calmly. "Ohhhhhh," Kablewy Bear sighed.

Lickin' Larry explained all the happenings of the day to his bear-friend and soon Kablewy Bear understood it all. "It was very considerate of you to not want to wake me up. Thank you for that. Say, do you know what time it is?" Kablewy finished.

Lickin' Larry found the smiling, yellow sun in the sky and said, "It is about noon...why do you ask Kablewy?"

"Noon!" Kablewy Bear shouted. "I'm late for work! I've got to go home and change! See you later! Bye Lickin' Larry!" and just like that he stumbled and bumbled his way into the long prairie grasses and headed for his den.

Chapter 6: A Lesson Learned

Curiosity suddenly gripped Lickin' Larry's little mind and he decided to follow his bear-friend. He found Kablewy Bear rushing out of his den dressed in a brown uniform with a shiny badge and he was wearing a brown, wide-brimmed hat.

"I did not know you had a job Kablewy," Lickin' Larry said to his bear-friend. "What is it anyway?" he asked. "Well, it's not a job per say..." Kablewy Bear answered, "I mean...it's like a job, but not a real job. It's a pretend job."

A puzzled look came across Lickin' Larry's little lizard face and Kablewy

Bear could see that his little lizard-friend was in need of more explanation.

"I'm dressed like this because I want the humans to think I'm a forest ranger," Kablewy Bear said. "What is a forest ranger?" Lickin' Larry queried. Kablewy Bear responded, "Forest rangers are the humans who make sure the other humans visiting our forest are safe. They also make sure those visitors respect our forest by following the rules. The visitors know the forest rangers are here to make sure things are good and so they show their appreciation."

"What do you mean?" Lickin' Larry

asked. His bear-friend answered, "Well, the forest rangers walk around in our beautiful forest all day taking care of this and taking care of that.

They check on the visitors and help them when it is necessary. So, as a thank-you the visitors will offer the forest rangers free meals most of the time. The other humans just feed them!"

"Wow...that is pretty interesting," Lickin' Larry noted. "Yeah! That's exactly what I thought and that's why I decided to get this uniform, shiny badge, and this big, round hat. I figured why should I work hard looking for food when I can just pretend to be a forest ranger and get it for free?!" Kablewy Bear added.

Lickin' Larry thought deeply about what his bear-friend had just told him and he felt compelled to tell Kablewy Bear the following because as we all know honesty is always the best policy. "Hey, Kablewy can we talk?" he politely asked.

Kablewy Bear could hear the sincerity in his little lizard-friend's voice and he suddenly forgot that he was in a hurry. He said, "Yeah, sure thing little, buddy...what's up?"

Lickin' Larry started talking to his

very good bear-friend and said, "I do not think that what you are doing is right." Kablewy Bear was intrigued by his little lizard-friend's words and asked, "Why not?"

"Well..." began Lickin' Larry, "you are lying to others by pretending to be something you are not and you are doing it so that you can get something from them. It is like you are taking advantage of their kindness and that is not right Kablewy. You are a better bear than that. How would you feel if someone were taking advantage of your kindness?"

Kablewy Bear listened intently to his

little lizard-friend because he had always known Lickin' Larry to be honest and respectful to everyone. He took the time to let the words sink straight into his big, bear heart and realized that Lickin' Larry was absolutely right.

He picked up his little lizard-friend and gave him a big, fat, gentle bear hug. Lickin' Larry sank into his furry and warm body and Kablewy Bear said to him, "Thank you for helping me to realize that what I was doing is wrong. Thank you from the bottom of my heart because you're right. I **am** a better bear than that. I'm very lucky to have your friendship and I will always be grateful for it."

After Kablewy Bear finished saying these words to his little lizard-friend he gently placed him back onto the ground. Lickin' Larry looked up into bear-friend's big, brown eyes and said, "Thank you Kablewy for being patient enough to think about what I said. I care about you and I only wish for you to be the best bear you could possibly be."

"And I will never forget to always remember that!" exclaimed Kablewy Bear. He tore off his uniform and tossed his big hat into the wind. It flew like a frisbee floating far away into the sky. "I think I'll go to the stream and do some fishing. Want to come?" he asked Lickin' Larry.

"No thank you Kablewy. I am still on a quest to search for Peanut Butter & Rock ice cream and that means heading towards Johnny's house which is in the opposite direction."

"Okie dokie...I'll see you another day then Lickin' Larry! Bye!" called out Kablewy Bear.

"Alright Kablewy have fun fishing! Bye, bye!" responded Lickin' Larry in kind and the two friends went their separate ways.

Chapter 7: Jackpot!

Petunia Pass was clear as could be and Lickin' Larry was happy to be on his way again. He had enjoyed his visit with Kablewy Bear and was proud of the positive choice his bear-friend had made. The happiness of it all gave him a spring in his step and he whistled his way to Johnny Jump-Up's house.

He came to a bend and remembered that his grasshopper-friend's house was just around the other side. Lickin' Larry hoped with all his might that Johnny would be there to welcome him.

Johnny's house was carved into the side of a tiny, tiny mound. It looked like half a bubble growing out of the ground. The colorful wild flowers decorating it made it seem like a painted canvas of blues, yellows, and greens.

Lickin' Larry quickened his steps even more. He wished he could fly... his legs were rolling like before when he left Sammy Spider's Store. He chugged like a train and picked up more and more speed because if you remember it was Peanut Butter & Rock ice cream of which he was in need.

He found his good friend relaxing under the porch. Johnny was swinging on a swing and singing a song called

"Light Up the Torch!" Lickin' Larry said hello to his grasshopper-friend and proceeded to tell him his day's story to the end.

Johnny was very impressed by Lickin' Larry's journey and asked his little lizard-friend, "In that case for Peanut Butter & Rock ice cream won't you join me?"

A smile so wide grew across Lickin' Larry's little face and he felt himself quite lucky to have a friend of such beautiful grace. "Of course I will join you!" exclaimed Lickin' Larry. Then into his house Johnny jumped happily.

He returned with two bowls with the

tastiest of treats and gave one to his friend so that they both could eat. Lickin' Larry said to his friend, "I just love Peanut Butter & Rock ice cream. Every time I have some I feel like I am in a dream."

They spent the rest of the day enjoying each other's company and watched the sunset in the distant valley. The light of the day soon faded away and the moon awaked in the sky. The two friends talked and sang of the golden days ahead and of those that had gone by. They talked and sang so much they did not realize how quickly time did fly! The time had come to go to

bed and each of them had a fluffy,
marshmallowy pillow upon which to
rest their head.

In their cots they fell asleep on
opposite sides of the room. The
windows were open so the breeze could
kiss them and so they could be watched
by the moon.

In the TV of their night heads did
the two friends have beautiful dreams
of how wonderful it was to be able to
share adventure, kindness, and
friendship over the wonder that was
Peanut Butter & Rock Ice Cream.

THE END

Made in the USA
Middletown, DE
08 November 2021